Denis Robert is a French journal............................ist and film
director. He is highly regarded for uncovering political and
financial scandals and for his unconventional journalism.
Happiness is his first novel. He lives in Paris.

Happiness

Denis Robert

Translated by John Innes

A complete catalogue record for this book can be obtained from the
British Library on request

The right of Denis Robert to be identified as the author of this work
has been asserted by him in accordance with the Copyright, Designs
and Patents Act 1988

Copyright © 2000 Les Arenes
Translation copyright © 2009 John Innes

First published as *Le Bonheur* in 2000 by Les Arenes, Paris

First published in this translation in 2009 by Serpent's Tail,
an imprint of Profile Books Ltd
3A Exmouth House
Pine Street
London EC1R 0JH
website: www.serpentstail.com

ISBN 978 1 85242 959 1

Designed and typeset by Sue Lamble

Printed and bound in Great Britain by
CPI Bookmarque Ltd, Croydon, Surrey

10 9 8 7 6 5 4 3 2 1

Why is your mind so occupied with sex? Because that is a way of ultimate escape. It is a way of complete self-forgetfulness. For the time being, at least for that moment, you can forget yourself – and there is no other way of forgetting yourself... When there is only one thing in your life that is an avenue to ultimate escape... you cling to it because that is the only moment you are happy. Every other issue you touch becomes a nightmare... so you cling to the one thing that gives complete self-forgetfulness, which you call happiness. But when you cling to it, it too becomes a nightmare, because then you want to be free from it; you do not want to be a slave to it.

Krishnamurti, *On Love and Loneliness*

We had a drink together outside a bar. She sat opposite me, smiling, not saying anything. It was chilly, she was wearing a short skirt. There were a lot of people around us on the terrace. She crossed her legs so high that I could see the white triangle of her pants. She noticed this. I knew that when she lowered her eyes, and pulled her skirt up even higher.

He attracted me, but I felt no desire for him. His freedom attracted me. That and his indifference. I was waiting to see what he would do. I didn't want to push things. I liked the way he spoke, pausing to think between each sentence, and the way he undressed me with his eyes. At the same time he had that shyness that makes you fear the worst.

Maybe he believed we met by chance. I was very self-conscious the first time.

She had read my books. People think writers like to be recognised, even admired. That was true of me at first. These days I prefer to be anonymous, to get on with my stories without having to answer to anybody.

At the time, I was dried up, blank. Not anxious, not depressed, just blank. I would have liked to be someone's ghost writer, to start all over again from scratch.

I had asked her to jot down her impressions in a little notebook. To keep a record of our meetings. I gave her the notebook as a present.

He never tried to seduce me. He wasn't particularly good-looking, by any fashionable criteria. He didn't seem to care about his appearance. A bit of middle-age spread, a nice smile. He wore shapeless velvet trousers, rollnecks and classic English leather shoes, and smoked an awful lot of unfiltered cigarettes. He drank house wine. No one could guess his real character. He wouldn't even know himself.

He wasn't the type to make the first move. He must have made up his mind that his wife was all he needed. He wasn't on the prowl, he was just looking.

Men think only of sex. Some admit it, but they're rare. Usually they don't practise it much. Others admit it to themselves and don't talk about it. They dream up all sorts of steamy scenarios without ever making them real. He thought about it, talked about it, and practised it.

She wasn't doing much with her life. Literary studies, unfinished. Freelancing, secretarial work, the odd book started and abandoned. I couldn't understand what she wanted from me. She already had that air of passivity and availability, a kind of self-sacrificial quality.

Something happened quickly with her which I find hard to define. With her, there didn't seem to be any danger.

I like to look beautiful but I am not so sure that I do. I've got pretty legs, very pale skin, a little wrinkle at the corner of my left eye, decent breasts. If you looked hard you could spot a bit of fat at the top of my thighs. I look very good in jeans. I had got by till then without worrying too much about how men perceived me.

'Hello, it's me, from the other day in the café – you remember?'

'Of course I do, how are you?'

'Very well, and you?'

'Not much happening.'

'It's about that piece of work on psychoanalysis that I have to deliver soon…'

I felt a bit stupid. I was breathless on the phone. That's how it always is when I'm impressed. He was polite, distant too. I called him the next day for some details. And then I left my number. I have never been able to call him without this fear in my stomach.

I asked myself what she saw in me. I thought it was because of books. The fascination of a writer. But I was wrong. Maybe it was money? If I had been poor, none of this would have been possible. But money, in the end, didn't interest her.

From quite early on I wanted to play a game with her. I didn't want an ordinary affair. Seducing women is tiresome. There is something predictable and depressing about making an effort to be wonderfully witty and attractive just so you can end up in bed with someone and stick your cock in their pussy. Dangerous and unprofitable, that's what I thought of infidelity.

This was something else.

I was certain he would call me. I don't think I doubted it for a moment. The knowledge that he had a wife and three children meant nothing to me. I expected nothing from him. I was available; I was up for anything. All I wanted was for him to take advantage of this.

I made him believe that my husband was a strong presence in my life. In fact my husband loved me like you love a piece of furniture. I had become something for display. My husband never asks questions. He is always working in the laboratory or travelling somewhere. I don't think my husband fucks other women. I think that sex has ceased to interest him, that he has buried the subject beneath a great heap of far more important concerns. He is making a mistake there. I have not yet found anything as serious as sex.

Between twenty and thirty-five, I was very dependent on my wife. I spent my time dreaming and writing. I tried to come home early.

A writer can only give what he has. Having never known hardship or cruelty, I could only be a kind of detached observer of everything that was falling apart around me. That's what I was paid for. My books, a few articles: my work left me sufficient freedom. For some time I had the feeling that I'd reached my limit. I started to come home late. I waited for better days.

It wasn't him who called me but a girlfriend. I got myself ready. Short skirt, strapless bra. Make-up by Shiseido. There was going to be a little party in a restaurant. I knew he'd be there. I knew he'd arranged it so that I'd be there.

I got a lot of attention during the evening. A boy in leather trousers, another in Armani, a piss-head with a fat cigar. He kept an eye on me from a distance. Just before he left, he gave me the address of his hotel and his room number. As if he was giving me his phone number.

'Here you are.'

'Thanks.'

We didn't exchange another word.

At this time, I did my work in a hotel room, as I often did when I needed complete seclusion in order to write. The hotel wasn't far from where I lived. Originally it had been my wife's idea: she had had enough of my bad moods at times like these. Starting a new book used to demand a lot of energy. With time, I have learned to go easier on myself. That particular evening everyone had been nice to me. My surly, asocial side didn't bother anyone. I got out of the restaurant quite early. I had left her my room number.

I masturbated while I was waiting for her. I often masturbate before fucking a woman I don't know. It helps me be more sure of myself, to allow pleasure to come more calmly. I masturbated into a white hotel towel and then slept while waiting for her to arrive.

I had spent the previous night channel-hopping on the television, having told my wife that I was working. On nights like these I often hunt for porn films on cable and masturbate while watching the screen. I sleep better after a good wank.

When she opened the door, I closed my eyes. I waited for her to come and push against me under the sheets. I didn't resist.

I had put the pack of condoms under the bed. I fucked her slowly, whispering stories in her ear. I wanted to turn her on. I was a bit drunk from vodka tonics.

I fixed a meeting with her for the next day. She seemed delighted. Her availability amazed me. She didn't ask any questions. Nor did I.

He started telling me stories straight away, his mouth against my ear. Words poured out, almost tenderly. When he penetrated me, his breath warmed me up. He told me of girls that do blow-jobs for cash, of bets involving sex and money, of strange places where lots of bodies can mingle together. Desire and fear.

Did he guess straight away that when I knelt before him, his cock in my mouth, the curve of my arse was simply an invitation to be penetrated? Did he perhaps understand straight away that my mouth, sucking so greedily on his fingers, already hoped for other cocks?

Perhaps he knew all that before I did? That day, I didn't say anything. I let his words flow over me.

What I liked most at the beginning was when she sucked me off. Not holding myself back. Never. Not thinking about her. Always hard. Letting her suck me as often as she wanted. She soon told me about her husband. I never encouraged her to do that again.

I must keep my distance. He fucked her on Sundays. From behind. While squeezing her breasts. She said it wasn't unpleasant and it was the least she owed him. Once, I think, I thought about my wife. I told myself that maybe she had a lover. I imagined her in bed with another guy. One of my friends. A couple cannot live off itself forever. Except by lying to themselves. Fidelity is a poor adhesive. An invention to make us believe that the two parties are bound together. But if you pull a bit, you know they come apart. The couple is based on a myth of fusion. As if together we make one. Whereas we are definitely two.

Women immediately know they're different. They don't need any time to adapt, any time to reflect. They know it, that's all. Men are much slower off the mark.

At the start you didn't matter much to me. I had noticed you, but there was something petty and provincial about you that got on my nerves.

For a week we made love as often as we could. We hardly slept. We never discussed different positions. We just fitted ourselves together naturally, even if the configurations were sometimes rather unusual. I said very little. Two or three sentences a day. My silence astonished him.

Had I already started to find it such a thrill to suck his cock?

This girl is crazy. I must find out more about her before going any further. When she looks at me, I feel like I'm under investigation.

What is it that makes me think about her all the time? To think about fucking her. To think about fucking her all the time. I must not phone her.

I spend a long time getting ready before I go and meet him. Even in normal times, make-up is a ritual for me, putting on a second skin to face the world and other people's eyes. When I'm 'in love' it's even more important. I can spend two whole hours on it. It reminds me of those women of the orient, whose bodies are bathed, whose hair is styled, whose cheeks are painted and powdered and who are carefully dressed before they are presented. My preparations are just like that: I make myself shine from head to toe. And then the waiting, which fills my stomach, a bit like climbing a staircase that goes on forever. The uniformed hotel porter gives me the key to the room, telling me that he hasn't arrived yet. He knows exactly what I've come here for. The word 'whore' crosses my mind. I prefer action to contemplation. With him, it doesn't take a lot. He only has to look at me to make me wet.

She lights a cigarette and tells me about her mother. I listen politely, while doodling on a piece of white paper that I've folded in half. I do that mechanically. Often. Observing, listening distractedly to her saying that fidelity is a lot of rubbish, She wants my assent. I'm somewhere else. All of a sudden I trust her. Yet something bothers me about the way she keeps looking at me. I'm suspicious, but intrigued.

I carefully keep all his little drawings. They're often funny, and very erotic. If he leaves me one day I could send them to his wife.

No, I'll never do that.

I kept making notes about her. Especially at the start. I even filmed her, without telling her, on one of our first nights. I put a camcorder on the chest of drawers. The light was poor, but you can still make out her body. You can see her quite clearly sitting astride me. And hear her words.

You're very crude when you're getting fucked. You like to be dominated. But I was rather quiet that time. I knew we were being spied on.

I replayed the film once and masturbated.

It wasn't the same after that, except for the first time when we watched it together and you laughed like mad.

I am trying to work out the difference between wanting someone and making love to him. I don't see it. Why wouldn't it be possible to love two people at once? Or three? At different moments? Why are lovers always so ungenerous to others?

I do not know where I am going with her.

After making love you often seem absent, as if you've with-
drawn into yourself.

I often wonder what you think of me.

I wonder if you do think of me.

I am not sure that I make you think.

There's something mechanical between us.

Something fateful.

I suggested that she buy a novel by Nicholson Baker. This was a few days after our first night. She had called me several times, always getting straight to the point. She wore flashy necklaces and rather short skirts. She had the voice of a child. She wanted me to recommend books that had impressed me. I told her about *Vox*. It's the complete transcript of a very long telephone conversation. The man and the woman will never see each other, but they turn themselves on via the handsets that connect them. A powerful erotic tension runs through the whole book, ending in an apotheosis.

It was a weekday, around noon. I had called him. I didn't know that his answerphone was recording us. He hadn't tried anything yet but he knew that he was on favourable ground with me.

It was very pleasant. I remember a conversation we had about films. You had come back from a weekend in the country with your husband. I wanted to know if you had read my book. We had still not talked about sex together. I was disturbed at the thought of you with this book. We discussed films very politely and then all of a sudden I asked you if you had read *Vox*. There was a silence and then you said 'Yes'. Then I asked you if you were wearing a bra, if it was a bit tight. I asked you to take it off. You hesitated, afraid that someone might come into the room. I suggested that you keep your blouse on. I wanted you to stroke yourself. Which you did. I could hear you breathing. During all this time we carried on talking about *Waterworld* with Kevin Kostner. The story of a mutant who grows lemon trees.

I was seeing you without seeing you. I saw your cock squeezed into your pants and the bulge that it made in your jeans.

'I spent yesterday in the country. I chopped up some logs.'

'You took the book with you?'

'Yes.'

'Was your husband there?'

'Yes, and his son and one of his friends, and the dogs. The 4x4 got stuck in the mud. We had quite a struggle getting the wheels free. You should have seen me... '

'Were you wearing rubber boots?'

'Why are you asking me that?'

'No reason. Just a question.'

'Tell me about your wife, how is she?'

'So-so. And your husband?'

'I don't like you talking about him like that.'

'You started it... When you were reading in the country, where was your husband?'

'Outside.'

'What were you wearing?'

'A baggy sweater and jeans.'

'Did you have bare feet?'

It was the first time I had spoken to her as 'tu' not 'vous'.

I could picture your hand getting to work on your cock while you thought of me. It made me hot, and proud.

'Did you carry on reading when your husband came back?'

'Yes, I made tea and we had some cake… '

'And then you… you moved to the bedroom?

'No, he was tired. That book put me in a funny mood. He must have seen me blushing. I picked up another book to cover my embarrassment.'

'What was it?'

'Blaise Cendrars, *Lice*. Do you know it? It's about his time in the trenches during the First World War, when he lost an arm… '

'What kind of bra are you wearing today?'

'Dark red, silk. And quite a low-cut blouse.'

'Isn't it a bit tight?'

'Yes, it is.'

'Take it off but keep the blouse on in case someone comes in.'

For thirty seconds the line is almost silent, just our breathing and the rustle of fabric, then her voice comes back on, a little hoarse.

I took off my bra. I couldn't bring myself to call you 'tu'. I had already done this ages ago with a boyfriend. He went too fast. But you were taking your time.

I asked you if you were still masturbating. You said 'Yes'. That was enough for me. We kept on for a good hour before you exploded.

We should have known from the start that everything we said and did and thought only existed for one thing. Sex. Not necessarily pleasure but, necessarily, sex.

We had our telephone period, before moving on to more serious things. The point of the game was always to try to go further. She put her trust in me. She thought I knew where we were going.

I've often worried about not being able to get an erection. After a night with her, I don't worry any more. But still, I don't love her. I mean, I am not in love with her.

At night I let you turn round and I snuggle into all the hollows that you make in your body. I could adjust to any movement you make but in fact you don't move much. I always hold your penis in my hand. It just lies there on my palm, fast asleep. Sometimes I feel it trembling a little and then I want to wrap my fingers round it again, to enclose it and start gently moving my hand. Up and down, up and down, pulling the skin, witnessing the miracle of blood flowing, feeling the veins swelling and knowing that this erection is for me. But I leave my fingers open because you must sleep. It is already very late.

One of my friends, Ernesto, thinks that what unites a man and a woman more than anything else is a perfect fit between their reproductive organs. Ernesto seriously believes that love is a biological lottery. His theory, which he never tires of repeating, is obscene. We've all seen ill-matched couples, a tall person with a short one, a beauty and a beast, so how do we explain this phenomenon? According to Ernesto, God dreamt up the idea of six or seven thousand million individuals with male and female connecting parts. Only a tiny proportion of sexual organs will properly match. This isn't a matter of size or depth, nor of movement. It's to do with something else. A chemical phenomenon. Hormonal magic. A matter of luck, blood temperature, moistening, bumps and hollows. Ernesto talks of 'capillarity'.

He also says that perfect happiness in a couple depends on sex.

'You fuck dozens of women in a lifetime, and they fuck dozens of men. How do you explain that love goes better with some than with others? It isn't just a matter of psychology. Sex rules. I can see that you've never understood that, or you wouldn't talk the way you do. You intellectualise too much. Let yourself go...'

Until I met you, I used to find this kind of conversation sterile. And Ernesto a bit of a moron.

No one at the publishing house knew what was going on between us. He turned up there yesterday, came over and stood behind me. There were a lot of people in the office. I was wearing the latest outfit that my husband had given me. The one with the zip at the back. Leaning over, he slipped his finger down between my pants and my skin. The zip was partly unfastened. He asked me to get up, then he went off to talk with his editor. When he returned he started again, pushing his finger in very deep. This was easier because I was standing up. I was dripping wet.

What I like best is the middle of the night, two or three o'clock. Did I move or did she suddenly remember I was there? You come close and pull the sheet down over my hips. Your arm slides over my stomach, your hand is still a bit cold. You mustn't wake me up, I mustn't turn over. You get closer still, I can feel the soft hair of your mound against my knee, you are so wet and open and I'm still not hard at all. You have to find your way between my legs, you rub yourself, and you gently push yourself into my dreams.

I am often shattered when I see her. I know that fucking is the only thing on her mind. Sometimes I am afraid I won't stay the distance. After the first blowjob, I'm confident. We fuck quarter of an hour later. And then again, one more time, before I fall asleep.

I also fuck my wife, intermittently.

I decide to spend a few days with my parents. My husband never comes with me. He's almost as old as my father. They have nothing to say to each other. For some months now, I've been thinking more often about my parents. I tell myself that maybe I've treated them unfairly. So I go, but as soon as I'm there I think only of getting away again.

I've blossomed. When I was leaving you said: 'How is it possible? You get more and more beautiful. Do I have this effect on you?'

I want to tell the world how happy I am to get myself fucked so well, that it's good for the complexion. I restrain myself a little.

I receive a great big bunch of roses. My sister doesn't give a damn, or pretends not to. My story of a married man with children sticks in her throat. She cannot help but project herself into the victim role, that of the woman betrayed and humiliated. She goes on about my husband, asks me if I ever think of how much I am hurting him. I tell her we only have one bloody life and that all I have to do is not tell him. I add that marriage doesn't vaccinate you against love, and nor does having children. I ask her if she's ever come more than once in a week. I know I'm being cruel.

I don't really believe in the love part of our story. It's a story and that's all there is to it. No one can blame me for being alive; I have no wish to hurt anyone. I am being absolutely realistic and I am not asking anything of him that he cannot give me.

I would like to explain to my sister that none of this is necessarily serious. I would like to warn her of the trouble that she's storing up for herself, with her head buried in the sand, a sanctimonious little old lady at the age of twenty-five, trotting out the same platitudes that they drummed into us when we were kids. I've never summoned up the courage to tell her that her husband played footsie with me last May, at Mum's place. I've never told her that I didn't resist. It takes a good stiff cock to make me lower my eyes.

I only did what he wanted.

I will never accept that there is anything bad in doing something good for yourself. There is only good.

Last Friday I gave her a vibrator. I'd had it gift-wrapped. I asked her to unwrap it after I left, after we'd had a good fuck. I would like to have seen her face at that moment. I'm sure she smiled. I am thinking of giving her others, increasing the size.

So many people with their heads in the sand. And such different heads, all ages, every religion, from the brightest to the dullest, all united in proclaiming that fidelity is the guarantee of love. Could I possibly be wrong about this? Could they possibly be lying? Why don't I blame myself? He tells me I'm perverse. I look at him, bewildered. Perverse? I grab the dictionary. So, it seems that I like to encourage evil. I am corrupt, depraved, debased, degenerate, diabolical. I am neither good nor virtuous. I display a deviation from basic instincts. I am bestial, exhibitionistic, fetishistic. I impulsively perform immoral acts. I am a masochist, a necrophile, a sadist, a voyeur, a zoophile. I seek physical pleasure outside the 'normal' sexual act. That is, outside heterosexual coupling between partners of reasonably equal age. I'll do anything.

What do I like best about her?

Her perversity. And her freedom. She is the freest woman I know. I am not telling her that I am starting to need her. I treat her badly.

My desire to make love with him seems quite natural to me. All the frustration of this secret relationship makes me incredibly greedy. It's quite impossible for me to fall asleep beside him. My hands just keep on wandering, and you'd have to tie me up to stop me touching him. I give him precious little rest but I refuse him nothing.

He says that the most exciting thing about me is the way I naturally accept every possible situation. I must in some way be a normal pervert.

I have no after-thoughts.

I'm a simple girl.

It's other people who make everything complicated.

The first time I saw her pushing in a vibrator and murmuring how good it was, I got an uncontrollable erection. Then she told me to masturbate. Which I did. I said to her: 'Turn round, show me your arse.' She stuck my big Montblanc pen in it.

And I masturbated all the harder.

Afterwards we went off for a pizza. The vibrator was hurting her. She asked me if she could take it out. Of course I said no.

I wanted him to say no. I came several times in the restaurant, especially when he pushed the vibrator with his foot, under the table. I think the waiter noticed. That turned me on even more. I wanted some device that could make time stand still. Then everyone in the restaurant would become a statue, except for him, and me, and the waiter. We would fuck on the table and the waiter would watch us and masturbate.

And then everything would go back to normal, but our eyes would be alight with something new and beautiful.

Something fiery.

I don't make too much of an effort with girls. That's what works, usually. I look at their arses a lot. They can be big, even huge. I am more demanding about arses than breasts.

I love to imagine a woman from behind, busy with something. I push her down, making her press her cheek against a table so that even when she's fucked she can see me fucking her. I push up her skirt to uncover her white, slightly flabby arse. I slap it with the palm of my hand, pull the cheeks apart and shove myself into her, using all my fingers to hold her reddening cheeks. I love white skin because you can see it get red. I'm not so fond of arses that are toned and bronzed, arses straight out of the gym, touched up with a fake tan. Arses like that aren't made for lovemaking, they're only made for show and for dance music. I worship white arses, those made only to be fucked.

It's just a matter of knowing how to talk to you to make you come, so I try harder and harder to entice you.

I tell you that I desperately need to feel your cock in my mouth.

It happened suddenly. Something clicked. Till I was thirty I cheated on my wife mainly in my head. I hardly ever thought about death. Let us say I was stuck in a rut, in a conventional world with no surprises, where happiness was hidden, never visible.

And then one summer night, while my wife was away on holiday, I picked up a hooker in the street. I was drunk. I took her to a hotel. I fucked like I hadn't fucked for a very long time. I paid her and made an appointment for the next day. This went on for a year.

I didn't know her name, she didn't know mine.

We must have screwed about thirty times in the year. That wasn't what I liked best. What I preferred was when she sucked me deep into her throat while rubbing her pussy. Her pussy was very hairy, very dark, very silky and shiny. In a year she must have sucked me off at least fifty times. I paid her thirty thousand francs.

We probably exchanged no more than a dozen words in all. I never knew why she played with herself. If she did it for me…

She taught me that there are sex stories and love stories and that it's a matter of building a great big barrier between them. And not talking about it too much. Which is what I did.

I can't stand useless talk. Empty words and hollow phrases make me really angry. Being awkward and hesitant leaves me cold. A man has a much bigger chance of getting what he wants by saying I really turn him on, that I make him so hard he'll burst out of his pants, than with stale chat-up lines. Shut your mouth and fuck me. Tell me you want to fuck me all night long. No one has ever spoken to me like that. And I've never spoken to anyone like that either. I suppose I don't look like the kind of person you can talk to so directly. With a lot of people they have scarcely opened their mouths and I can see the pathos of the whole situation. How can they be so naturally vapid? All too often I get trapped by my own curiosity. It makes them bold and then I have no end of trouble getting rid of them. I have a whole store of words ready to use. They fill my head and can never come out. You are the first to have understood.

In the evening we set off by car for Paris. I'm driving, and we're going very fast. She starts caressing me, to a point where we're soon in danger of having an accident. I ask her to wait a bit. I ask her to take off her pants and tights. Her skirt is pulled up, the tights pulled down over her red pumps. I push my fingers inside her. My right hand opens her lips to expose her clitoris, my fingers move round it, just skimming over it, then push back inside her. They're seeking out that warm, sticky fluid deep in her vagina.

I keep pushing in and out until the desire become unbearable, and her whole body arches up against my hand.

Her eyes dart back and forth between me and the road. She wants us to swap places. I refuse. I put both hands back on the steering wheel watching her caressing herself. I say to her: 'Go on, rub yourself hard.' I overtake trucks.

I push my thumb deep inside my cunt and force a finger into my anus. He's overtaking trucks and slowing down so they can enjoy the scene. I smile at such generosity. My index finger finally heeds the desperate call of my little button. My thumb and finger can feel each other through the delicate wall that separates my two organs, and I am going to come very soon and I want him to enjoy it too. The car park is only a few hundred metres away but my orgasm comes first. I don't give him time to stop, my hands are already tearing at his belt and I throw myself on him. My lips move right down along his length and then gently back up, accompanied by my hand, my tongue spreads that pretty little slit at the tip, I dribble with happiness on to it. That special voice of his gently penetrates me. He's telling me about someone who's approaching the car, no doubt the driver of the truck parked beside us. I make a move to raise my head but his hands push down on my neck to stop me and make me carry on with what I'm doing. He asks me to get close up against the window, to raise up my arse, and I shake my head, no, without stopping sucking him, suddenly I'm very scared. He tells me again to get close to the window, describes the guy, someone totally repulsive. I feel cold air. But I push my arse as high as I can. He opens the window wider. I don't know whether it's the cold or fear that is making me shudder most. I'm waiting feverishly for hands to be placed on me, for them to spread my cheeks and to be taken violently.

I am flowing with pleasure.

His sperm brings me back to reality as it floods my mouth. I roll it beneath my tongue before swallowing and sit up laughing. The car park is empty.

I have the feeling that I have nothing left but sex and her.

We drive on in silence. I play a tape of the same song over and over. Shirley Horn, *Trav'lin' Light*. I look at him from time to time. He smiles at me and I feel good.

His desire for me gives me a legitimacy that I've never found anywhere else. The feeling of having the right to be there. Were it possible, I would live with his cock permanently inside me.

I could be a perfect mistress if he wanted to have one.

She said to me: 'The two of us are going to have a great time.' I love that phrase. If we had got there a couple of hours earlier I'd have taken her straight to a club. I make an appointment with her for the following evening.

I wait for him all evening. He doesn't turn up, then phones at midnight to apologise. His wife.

The next day he calls me to fix a meeting in a smart restaurant near the Champs-Elysées. I get there first and insist on waiting on the pavement despite the entreaties of the porter who wants me to come inside. I look out of place with my pink mini-skirt and plaits. I am wearing dark glasses which partly hide my face and a long lambskin coat that I leave open. I imagine the kind of look I'd get from one of my husband's colleagues if he recognised me in this outfit.

Heads bowed together over our plates we tirelessly tell each other all our dirty stories. He's very polite and looks after me like a little girl. With his bare foot between my thighs he encourages me to eat. I must have taken at least an hour to finish my meal before he suggests we go off for a drink.

A discreet brass plate on a discreet door in a secluded street. She can guess what's going to happen. I've told her it will be hot. She squeezes my hand, asking me if I'm not worried that people will recognise us. To tell the truth it's never crossed my mind. In this place everyone is in the same boat. To reassure her I whisper that the hardest part is letting yourself go.

'And after that, it's just like riding a bike, you'll see… '

The door is opened, cautiously, a couple of inches. A quick check confirms that we meet the criteria of the establishment. All these places have the same rules: women are strictly forbidden from wearing trousers; rollnecks and other garments that cover up too much are strongly discouraged; single men are only allowed in at certain times or on certain evenings. Visits by single women are extremely welcome but highly unlikely.

We go and sit at the bar. The ceiling is too low, the light pallid; worn-out red velvet and Seventies music. Close-ups of fucking on the video screens. And photos of women with big tits, sleazy, old-fashioned pin-ups, except that here they're framed. I go off to have a look round. I can see her perched anxiously on her bar stool, trying to look calm and confident. Her eyes travel round the room and meet those of a few predators ready to pounce on the first prey they can find. I decide to let myself be distracted by the behaviour of the two waitresses, both completely shaved, wearing only strings and sparkling tassels. I return when she ought to be starting to curse me for leaving her all on her own. I take her into a darker part of the room.

We make a place for ourselves in the circle that has formed around two girls. They are lying on the floor, one on top of the

other, caressing each other to the sound of the Stones' *Angie*. A few guys are watching them, turned on, but mainly annoyed at not being able to join in. The boss of the club comes up and starts ranting about this slut who keeps taking his girls. The slut in question has stuck her head under the skirt of the other one and keeps brushing away the male hands that touch her.

I would rather like it if she did that to me. He has other plans for me, takes me into an adjoining room and makes me stand in front of a more inclusive couple. The woman keeps shouting 'Oh yeah, yeah, that's so good, go on, give it to me' as she writhes about under some bloke. I find the scene rather comic, but I'm not there to laugh.

It's a big room, with wide couches along three of the walls. A dim red light casts strange shadows on the bodies. He takes me into a corner and starts undressing me. My pants are soaked. A few people have followed us but still keep a respectful distance. I'm quickly naked and kneeling in front of him, rubbing myself while busy with him. It's really great to be watched. This is the first time. I turn my back to them but I can hear their breathing. That unmistakeable faint, squishy sound of masturbation tells me what they're doing. Soon they are touching me. How many different hands are exploring me? No way of telling, the body doesn't provide such information. It will only transmit messages of pleasure or pain, without one being able to really tell which is pain, and which is pleasure.

I watch her performing. I ask her to wank the other guy. She does as she's told. I didn't think she'd agree so quickly, I was expecting a bit of resistance.

My hand is suddenly lifted off his body and on to an unknown cock. I resist this surprise attack, rapidly withdrawing to familiar territory, the stranger's hand still grasping my wrist. That voice of his that's become so familiar to my ears and my orgasms asks me to masturbate the stranger. I am not a disobedient girl, I abandon all resistance, and even find some pleasure in making an organ come that is detached from any real person. It's a rather thick cock. I wank it off as best I can. I no longer know what's going to happen to me. I trust him. Completely.

His arms find me and lift me up to a better position. I have the impression of resurfacing after holding my breath under water for a long time. I'm a bit drunk and can't make out what's going on around me. I allow myself to be touched and stroked all over, and confidently meet all the eyes staring at me when he turns me round to face them. My eyes are open but I cannot distinguish the shapes. I feel strong and beautiful. Hands penetrate me all over. My head falls back and nestles against his shoulder, into the safety of his reassuring smell.

I am entering a new dimension that's hard to describe: a complete absence of any thoughts. The feeling that my mind is ruled by my body and all its sensations. Freedom I have never known, pride I cannot explain.

I pull her away from them just as they were definitely about to fuck her. One unhappy guy suggests that maybe she might have something to say about this. He looks at her waiting for an answer. I give him a scornful smile.

Me? Make a decision? He really hasn't grasped what's going on. Right now I wouldn't be able to decide how many lumps of sugar to put in my coffee. My pleasure is bound to my submission. The very fact he's speaking to me seems completely out of order.

Now I really want to fuck her.

I let myself be taken to one of the couches and we make love ignoring the place and its inhabitants. I am very grateful to him for telling me that he loves me at that moment.

I tell her that I love her. It isn't a future commitment, it's an unexpected declaration. It came out without any effort. Almost naturally. Normally I never say that. I wanted to thank her for being how she is. Afterwards, I recall that I regretted having said it to you.

That unexpected declaration frightened you. You told me you never said that. Even to your wife.

You were afraid that I'd seize on this 'I love you' like a victory, that I'd turn it against you.

You were afraid and you made me pay for it.

That was the point at which I asked myself why I was so unworthy of being loved by you.

She kisses me, opening her mouth wide. She's usually lazy with her tongue but this time she keeps it in my mouth for a long time. I let this pass and wait to see what will follow.

Next day on the phone she asks me to describe what had happened. She wants to know what I thought of her. She plays at not remembering any more. She just recalls the stairs and her fear.

'After that, it's a blur. How was I? Tell me.'

'You were very good… exactly as one should be. You were available, open to just about everything. I think that I could have done whatever I wanted with you.'

This trust scared me.

I'm happy with my body, though I wouldn't mind having slightly bigger breasts. My body will age. I am content to live as I do now. I won't be able to do this when I'm older. I do not know what love is. The versions of it that I get to see every day don't convince me. All that selfish, comforting dependency.

When I'm older I'll have these memories. I'll get fucked while recalling these moments. I only have to think back to the scene in the club to get wet.

When I am older I know you will not be there.

Sex is a drug. I switch between periods of indulgence and abstinence. There are days when I think about it so much that I can't concentrate on work or anything else. I want to write a porn novel.

A writer has complete impunity. People who have a writer in their midst must be aware that anything they say or do can be used by him. They know it.

You can do whatever you like with me. You won't manage to make me dislike you, however hard you try.

I'm caught in a trap. At first I thought I could use you in order to write.

I felt that our adventure could make a fine story, but I lack all perspective.

I keep urging her to record everything in her notebook.

I meet him at his home the following evening. His family have gone away for the weekend and he's decided to join them later. So he can spend an evening with me.

He's tired but pleased to see me. I've been feeling great and overexcited ever since he called me in the middle of the afternoon. When he opens the door he holds out tickets to a concert: I wrack my brains to try and remember who the singer is. No, her name doesn't ring any bell. He sighs, saying we're from different generations. The pleasure he takes in stressing our age difference makes me laugh. Our ten-year gap means little to me. He would love me to be even younger.

We are very late and I scarcely have time to say hello before we're off on his scooter. It's a very mild evening, the breeze blows up my skirt and reveals my pants to the delight of passing motorists. I cling on to him like a real girlfriend.

She'd never heard of Marianne Faithfull.

While we're riding along she's stroking me. I try not to ejaculate. The stain would be too obvious on my linen trousers. I try. And then I stop trying.

I adore it when someone makes love to me while I'm busy with something else. I try to hold my concentration for as long as possible: that really turns me on. The concert hall is packed solid, no chance of the tiniest little caress in this sardine tin. I annoy everyone trying to get to the front to see the singer. I try to get interested in what's happening on the stage, I try to listen to the music but my brain simply refuses to focus on anything but him for more than a couple of minutes. He's too far away from me and so I end up going back to him. I kiss and hug him a bit, draw him out of the light. There's not enough space. People cough. He asks me if I'm enjoying it. I say 'Yes, yes' without much enthusiasm. My to-ing and fro-ing starts to get on people's nerves. We decide to leave, to general approval. I rub his cock on the exit stairs. I feel it swelling beneath my fingers through the thin fabric. He rubs himself against my arse in the gloom.

On the way out a friend notices the stain on my trousers. I am a bit embarrassed. He smiles. I can see that he finds her beautiful.

Now that Saturday night outs have become rather low-life, Fridays are the hottest nights of the week. Swinger clubs follow the same principle. After midnight, everyone wants a bit of human warmth. And more than that, if they find the right person. I'm starting to like this new place where he's taken me – it's a younger crowd and the women are better looking.

The basement is like a labyrinth. It's oppressively hot and sticky. Narrow corridors connect rooms of different sizes, their stone walls making me think of some medieval castle or dungeon. A woman with Afro braids, her eyes hidden behind dark glasses and her arse squeezed into a Jean-Paul Gaultier leather skirt, sits astride a guy with his trousers down. Her skirt is unbuttoned to the top of her thighs, but none of the little straps on her red bustier is unfastened. I can't see the man's face yet. But she is dazzling. She keeps her back straight, leans her head slightly forwards, her braids alternately covering and revealing her face. I come closer. Completely absorbed in the rhythmic movements of her pelvis, she seems hardly to notice us as we settle down at a distance which leaves little doubt as to our intentions. Her friend welcomes us with a smile.

Copying perfectly, she half-undresses, removes her skirt and pants, opens her waistcoat but keeps her bra on which increases the size of her breasts. They overflow a little from the bra and to excite her I pinch the exposed flesh. She climbs on to me. I penetrate her straight away, very hard and very deep.

I really want him to fuck me in the arse.

I am afraid of ejaculating too quickly. While she's monopolising my cock I snort some poppers. The fumes help you to stay focussed, and to feel your skin like a second coating of rubber. To take that tiny distance that allows me to stay aware of the pleasure that it will be to come inside her. To postpone and extend the moment when, inevitably, I am going to explode.

I rest the spread cheeks of my arse on his cock and push myself down on to it very gently. He keeps absolutely still, letting me gauge precisely my pleasure and pain. I stop breathing. His advance into this tight little corridor isn't achieved without difficulty and I let him go in and out ensuring that each time he gets a little further. When at last no more resistance prevents his advance, he decided to come alive again. He takes my hand and puts it on my arse. He shows me how much I've opened up for him. I would have found it hard to imagine that. My anus is a big open flower, as sweet as whipped cream. I get him to come back inside, I want him to go really deep. The feeling of emptiness that I discover in my stomach drives me crazy. My neighbour leans over to remind me of his existence. His fingers explore the abandoned place.

I turn round to them and it's like looking at myself in a mirror. The girl has removed her bustier. My hand reaches out to her to check the accuracy of the picture. The reality fills me with delight; perfectly synchronised sodomy.

I say to her:

'You were made for sex, you should do nothing else.'

She replies:

'Don't forget to make love to me tomorrow before leaving.'

She said that to me just before falling asleep. Her tired eyes, her body crying out for rest. How could I forget?

Why does she seem so amorous?

Earlier on at the bar she kissed me and held me in her arms under the bewildered eyes of the guy who had just been fucking her. I don't think she recognised him.

With her I'd dare anything.

She's my best friend. She's just told me the latest story about her boyfriend. He wanted to organise some swopping with friends and only needed her OK to fix a date. Her reaction makes it clear that it isn't something she'd consider in her wildest fantasies. I ask her why it's so horrible to sleep with people you don't know. She looks at me in disgust, then in amusement. She's sure I'm joking, just to wind her up. It calms me down a bit to see her just when I was starting to think that the whole world only dreams of one vast huge orgy. I wonder whether her boyfriend's proposal was meant seriously. I dare not imagine the start of an argument about the question. An argument about what, in fact?

I feel I'm different.

I don't experience the slightest shame at going to swinger clubs, merely an ever wider detachment from the mass of conventional couples. I'm not trying to scandalise anyone. I'm just asking myself a few questions about sexual fantasies and practices. I do not accept rules, I have no absolute principles, and I'm not going to let anyone impose a morality on me which isn't mine. The prohibition of sodomy in certain US states makes me laugh out loud. For a democratic state to try and legislate on the sexual proclivities of free adults – that's something truly surreal.

For the first time since we got to know each other, we're a bit bored. The clubs are always the same, after a few evenings you feel you know it all, you know in advance what's going to happen. I wonder what new thing I can invent to please her. I suggest she offers me one of her friends. Or two. She refuses, shocked.

When you arrive soon I will be on the balcony watching the passers-by in the street. The door will be ajar; you will come in without making a sound. You will press against me from behind without anyone being able to see you, and you will lift my skirt. You'll hold your penis against me and you'll stroke me through my pants. I'll arch my back, you will push hard against me. You'll rub yourself against the fabric until you can feel that I'm good and ready. Then I'll call down to someone in the street. At that precise moment you will push aside my pants to penetrate me. I'll choose someone walking his dog and I'll tell him about how much all the dog shit on the pavements is costing the community. I'll keep talking until my voice cracks with pleasure. I'll try to keep going as long as possible. It's got to be violent and intense. One day I realised how much power I had over you.

She talks to me about Clinton, and Monica's lips. The discussion wanders off into how we are conditioned, and the way sex is portrayed in American films.

You can dedicate your whole life to sex, dream of nothing else, even keep a permanent erection. Become a preacher, a procurer, a pornographer. She says she'd like to be a little mouse so she could creep into the bedroom of Kenneth Starr.

She prefers the Russians. Definitely.

My husband is away in the USA. I'm spending two long weeks out of town. Back at my parents. You are on holiday with your wife and children. You told me before leaving that I must have a good time and not think too much about you.

I try to follow your advice, without much enthusiasm. I sleep with one of your t-shirts which loses your smell as the nights pass. I catch up with old friends, take stock. Twenty-nine, a husband who is more and more like a ghost, an occasional lover (you) who phones me regularly, talks very quietly and tells me he has to hang up now.

Twenty-nine years old and how many lovers so far? I no longer know how to count, I don't know who I should count. Does a blowjob count? A blowjob doesn't mean anything, say the Americans.

Twenty-nine and how many blowjobs?

I go out every evening. My father doesn't understand. He disapproves. The same hard look, the same little command: 'Don't come back too late.' It's nearly ten years since I left the family home. Nearly thirty years of my father's disapproval. And my mother who keeps her mouth shut, as she always has. One day I am going to tell them about everything they've screwed up. Starting with me.

A philosophy lecturer is flirting with me. He's sweet. He invites me to a restaurant, chats me up. I surprise myself by asking him if he wants to fuck me. I would never have been so blunt in the past. He's a bit put out by this. I hardly have the time to start fondling him before he comes in my hand. He apologises, says it's never happened to him before. When at last he fucks me I excite myself even more by thinking of you.

I take advantage of the holiday to fix the roof, which has started to leak. I rediscover the joys of do-it-yourself. An empty mind. I've brought along some books of Indian philosophy. I fall asleep after reading a few lines. The sea is blue. The house is white. The TV is on all the time. My daughters make necklaces from shells. The taller one has a boyfriend who wears torn jeans and has an earring. My wife is absent and my daughters are too grown-up. In the evenings I wander around with the dog. I watch the waves rise and fall. And then rise. And then fall.

I get my feet wet. I don't go swimming. I go to the beach. I bring them chilled water and cakes and then I go back to the house. I listen to the Tour de France on the radio. In the evenings I open a bottle of white which I always finish. I still don't like whelks. I think of you when I'm fucking. I see you sweating on your vibrator. My wife is very pleased with what I'm doing, 'The holiday is doing you good', she says. I give her a smile and kiss her shoulder.

I return before he does. I'm sulking because I can't speak to him. My husband is very attentive. He shows me an article he's published in an American scientific review. He's evidently very proud of it. We go to a fancy restaurant. That same evening my husband fucks me for the first time in two months. I don't feel anything in particular.

I've been waiting for your phone call for several days. Your voice is warm. I want you. I ask if you've missed me. You avoid answering. You quickly draw me into my tales of sex. I tell you how the other evening I went to the birthday party of one of my girlfriends. I knew hardly anyone. I didn't feel like chatting. I felt like getting drunk. It was a jolly party – champagne, petits fours, old disco tunes. Almost all the girls were blondes, heads high, looking proud. I wonder what they do to be so sure of themselves. Someone put on some Cuban music. I found myself in the arms of a guy who pulled me into a backbeat dance where the movements were explicitly sexual. After a moment I asked him why he was going so fast. He looked at me in astonishment then asked me to follow him. He led me into the car park opposite the flat and fucked me on the bonnet of a car. The car was very dirty and I could feel the heat from the engine warming my arse. A lot of people passed by. We had to finish off a bit further away against a wall. I kept my eyes closed throughout, I didn't want to see him, I thought of you, and I had a very long orgasm. Then I went home to bed. He returned to the party; I think his girlfriend was there.

I ask her if she can find a pretext for us to spend three days together.

I'm finishing my book. My publisher is happy. No one in my circle has any suspicion of my parallel life with her. I'm a responsible, well-adjusted, monogamous citizen. I never talk about sex in public.

I use the excuse of a family reunion to take a long weekend. Then I phone my mother to explain that I've got too much work to spend two days away. These lies appal me.

The two hours before I see him allow me time to daydream. I want to undress, to be an exhibitionist, to make him hard just by moving. I can easily imagine his eyes taking me in, his little encouraging smile. I can picture my movements perfectly: my hands running up my thighs, dragging my ridiculously short skirt with them, the swing of my hips and my shoulders, my head thrown back and my hair touching him when I turn round to show him my other side. My fingers slipping under the elastic of my skirt and making it fall. My thong which goes the same way. My red nails making ten little marks on my white buttocks when I begin to stroke myself. My body bent forward so he can push himself in between my breasts, deep, like my smile.

When she enters my office, which luckily is empty at this late hour of the evening, I throw myself on her without bothering to say hello. I pull up her skirt, ask her to turn round. She puts her arms on the wall. I screw her quickly, not bothering whether she's enjoying it. I bang away and come very fast. She turns round and bites my shoulder till the blood comes.

I don't mind being welcomed like this, indeed I find his assault rather pleasant after these weeks apart. I protest vaguely, just for form's sake. He asks me if I'm not afraid of getting raped going around dressed like that. It never crossed my mind. My outfits are intended for him. I see myself through his eyes.

I came too fast. She would like me to get hard again. We play around a bit. I let the phone keep ringing until someone knocks on the door. I ask them to wait. I make her hide in the cupboard, and stick her skirt under my sweater. My seven o'clock appointment comes in.

I'm squatting down in the cupboard. His sperm trickles out on to some newspaper. My arse will be black. His voice lulls me. Once my mother watched me while I was trying on clothes in front of the mirror: a little black dress and knee-high suede boots. I turned and asked her what she thought. She answered very politely that it was perhaps a bit 'tarty'. I smiled, only too happy that we agreed.

I've nothing else to do in this cupboard but play with myself and doze.

I can hear my mother's laugh. We're in her little green car. I'm about nine years old. Her laugh when she said: 'What? You don't know what getting hard means?' My girlfriend didn't know either. We hadn't encountered the word, despite our sex education classes. My mother laughed, but didn't explain anything. The next year, during dictation, there was fat Ludo, the one who always came to school in a tracksuit. I was sitting next to him. A gleam in his eye, and a nudge with his elbow: 'Look, I've got a hard-on'. It took that bulge in his velveteen tracksuit pants for me to understand my mother's laugh. Ludo had spots and yellow teeth. And I made him hard. So young.

I let the interview run on for an hour. I enjoy thinking about her, with my hands in the deep pockets of my trousers. Letting the bloke talk, I touch myself to check. Still hard. When he leaves I open the cupboard door. She smiles at me. She stretches her bare legs. She howls with pain. Cramp. She says I'm a complete bastard to make her suffer like that. Arse in the air, she throws punches into space. I catch her fists and stick my tongue in her mouth. She doesn't resist. I make her bend down in front of me. I unpack my cock, stiff with waiting.

He sometimes talks to me about prostitution. He says he could sell me to friends or wealthy strangers. Realising that it is possible for me to earn money with my body sends me off into a trance. I've always been fascinated by prostitution. The lack of emotion reassures me. Not to be obliged to feel affection, to be free of any attachment, to become an object to be used and with a price, all that lifts a great weight from me. I am not so sure that emotions are necessarily forgotten in relationships like this. The absence of constraints gives a greater freedom, opens the door to a different form of love.

I am thinking of my friend Ernesto. He would pay to have her, I'm sure. I think she'd like that. He mustn't know that I know her. And then she will tell me all about it. Ernesto is going to marry a girl from Neuilly. Lots of money, great arse.

In the end, I think he'd rather give me away than sell me. When we return in the early hours, after our little tour of the clubs, he tells me that a friend is sleeping at his place and he'd like me to go and join him in his bed. The idea of being apart from him for even a minute doesn't exactly fill me with joy. I feel lost if he doesn't participate, even just by watching, in shows that are put on just for him. I find it hard to imagine what kind of pleasure he could get by imagining me with his friend. Perhaps he wouldn't get any? I hope at least that his satisfaction will be in proportion to the obedience that he's managed to get from me.

She looks sullen in the morning.

'So how was it?'

'It was crap, total crap.'

'Yes? Why? What happened?'

'Why didn't you come?'

'I couldn't. I don't want to fuck with friends. And I am sure you enjoyed yourselves.'

'That's one way of putting it... I tried to make him hard but he was embarrassed by the situation. I am not sure he appreciated your wedding present. It put him off to know you were next door. You ought to have gone out.'

'It's my home, after all.'

'I don't care. If you had really wanted to please him, you shouldn't have stayed here. You either had to come, or go.'

I don't feel anything in particular. I feel empty. Not jealous or worried, not excited at the idea of knowing she was fucking someone else. I think I did it to test her obedience. To know that she is so submissive is a little disturbing. Just how far does she want me to go? How far can she go?

Twenty centimetres long, twelve in circumference, my new vibrator is rather well proportioned. It never breaks down, you can count on it 24 hours a day. You can even, if you so desire, dress it in a real false skin in pink latex which takes perfection to the point of imitating the swollen veins of an erect penis. It has an adjustable gentle vibration, which is very pleasant if you manage to ignore the fact that it sounds like an electric mixer when you switch it on.

She asks me if she is supposed to laugh or cry at a gift which heralds lonely nights. I tell her that we have to see each other less often because my wife and daughters are back. I take her to the video shelves to choose a film that we can watch in the sex shop cubicle, while waiting for the peep show to start.

I'm ignorant when it comes to pornography. The only time I've ever seen a film of that genre was in my early teens. I was on holiday with my aunt and uncle. I was about as virginal as you could be at this time and they had quite a row about whether they should let me watch such a film. Opinions were divided between fear of shocking me, wanting to make me happy, and trying to help with my education. For an hour I listened to them argue, telling me at the same time that they wouldn't dare send me to bed. I was thirteen or fourteen. They had rented a vaguely pornographic film. A story about young girls at a boarding-school knocking off the gardener. When I think back to it, I feel rather uncomfortable and I can't understand what the pleasure was for them. Watching a porn film with the family, what a bizarre idea! I remember being disappointed when, right in the middle of the story, my uncle turned off the TV. The gardener must have got his tool out. I went to bed reluctantly. I don't think I really felt any pleasure. Vulgarity has a disastrous effect on my libido. Tongues hanging out, obscene expressions on faces, and the dialogue, especially the dialogue, was really awful. 'Leave a bit for your pal.' Two girls sharing a cock and a guy as thick as two short planks. Yuk.

As far as I can remember it was a German film. The girls had white breasts and bore the marks left by their pants and bras. I watched it when my parents were out. I also bought some shrink-wrapped Danish books that I hid in the attic. My mother asked my father why I spent so much time up there. 'Leave him be, he's just clearing up', said my father. Between thirteen and fifteen I must have jerked off a thousand times. Later, other hands helped me. My parents never talked about sex in the house, or only jokingly. Sex and its representations were forbidden. Banished. Buried. You either had to live without it or make it a subject for belly laughter. The dirtier the laughter, the better.

Bodies in action fascinate me. In the sex shop you are sitting beside me, with your skirt up, and your smile. We're warming ourselves up by first watching a video. I find you beautiful. I like watching you enjoying these forbidden images. It's a real little treat.

It's time for the six o'clock show. The curtain rises. On the stage a woman with lifeless skin slowly takes her clothes off. She wears a wig as dark as her glasses. Three men in pleated trousers have got their penises out and are masturbating as they circle round her. Hands rubbing, stroking, touching, pushing. All the cocks stretching out towards this one woman.

We try the vibrator in all positions and every speed. On my clit, between my lips. In front. Behind. With Vaseline. In my mouth, without its skin – that's not bad. The cocks ejaculate one after another on the body of the woman in the wig. Her stomach and face are covered in long, white slicks. I would like to be in her place.

In China, the masters of Tai Chi teach their disciples that avoiding ejaculation prolongs life. We have to store up this nourishing sap, this life-giving energy.

I will die young and wrinkled.

He's tired and morose. I'm grumbling. We have our first quarrel. Like a lot of men, he devotes a great deal of his life to his work. It's become a job like any other. He lives off it. I can feel he's tense, drowning in contrary currents. Yesterday he told me he hadn't seen his daughters growing up. That's not my problem. The only time I get from him is between midnight and five in the morning. He doesn't know me any better than he knows them. What could he say about me? I'm a good fuck. I give good head. I'll do anything with nothing in return. One day he told me that I was someone very rare. It was supposed to be a compliment. Our three days are reduced to two. He decides to go away, I don't know where, or for how long. He is very sorry, he can't do anything else. I think he likes seeing me deeply affected. Hurt. Having believed I was hard as steel, he now sees I'm vulnerable.

I told her that deriving great pleasure from making love with someone isn't the same as loving them. When I leave she cries for the first time.

I've known for a long time that I'm not cut out for happiness. I only have peaceful moments in between long periods of self-analysis. None of this has anything to do with him. To see me weak reassures and flatters him. He doesn't know what stance to take faced with my sudden outburst of emotion. Where did I go to find all these reserves of pain?

My dependency is first of all a physical one. Our game has driven me crazy. When I feel I may lose him I get withdrawal symptoms. I can't do anything to prevent this anxiety. I don't know whether I love him or don't love him. I don't care. He blocks out all reflection on the subject. He's my needle, and my cancer, and my fuel. He makes my life exciting.

You've become like a hard drug. You make me forget everything else. You create a fog. You stop me seeing the world around me. You stop me living. You are eating me up from inside. You disgust me. You understand?

I'm asking myself how you've managed to make me such a slut. I didn't have any particular tendencies in that direction. Today you want me to see other men, you don't want me to get attached…

My dependency only reveals yours.

My husband is away more and more. I go out with a journalist to pass the time. He takes me to the theatre. He's very kind and patient, can spend two hours talking to me about Italian neo-realism. I met him in the Métro. I was looking at a poster with the week's cinema listings, and he gave me an animated critique of every film on offer. He asked me to join him and some friends for a meal at their place; I agreed to come and have a drink. I left him two hours later with his phone number scribbled on a beer mat. I waited until I had heard nothing from you for three weeks before calling him.

In the interval at the theatre I rush off to phone you. You ask me to come and join you straight away, although you know very well I am with someone. I try to persuade you to wait for a couple of hours but you're not having it. I go back to him and explain that I'm terribly sorry but I absolutely have to go, that it is very important for me.

Those are my words, my own words: 'Very important for me.'

I leave him standing there before he has time to answer. Are all the nights with you worth these humiliations?

Sex needs lies and secrets in order to survive against everything else. There are my daughters, my wife, my plans, the books, the ones I've read, the ones I've still to read and to write, my memories, my friends, my last illusions, the sport that I have to play if I want to avoid a heart attack. There are dinners at home drooling over the X.X.O. cognac swilling around in the bottom of our fat balloon glasses. There is cocaine. There is the endless, weary repetition of things and ideas. There is the obvious absence of freedom. Boring conversations with friends. My wife going on about her wrinkles and that new liposuction cream that she's just bought at the gym, and that painter who's so charming – oh, what's his name, you know, Claude's friend? No, I don't know and I don't give a shit. There is my non-existence and the fact that I don't really know any more what will become of me. The way you look at me is the best thing that has happened for a long time.

I exist in your words and through your caresses. I don't control my body. I submit totally and unreservedly to your will.

The gift of my body is just a form of exchange.

It's only fair.

Our pursuit of pleasure is something fragile, it depends entirely on us and our psychological inclinations. Our bodies go into action later on. Contrary to the beliefs of novice voyeurs, there is nothing mechanical about it. This search for danger, this certainty that tomorrow it'll be over, and this permanent transgression of all the codes of love – is absolutely thrilling.

With her, I can't see any prohibitions.

Some nights I'd even fuck a tree. Thinking of you.

In my case, it's the tree that would fuck me. If it had your scent.

I couldn't live with a girl like her. If her husband and my wife didn't exist, our story wouldn't exist either.

An erect penis pointing up at me is a proof of love. I sometimes feel that very deeply yet I have never confused sex and love. I even persist in wanting to separate them, with dubious determination.

Sometimes I shake myself and ask if I really like you. You have never done anything to make me like you. You've never shown me more than one side of you. The sexual side.

I am finding it harder and harder not to feel guilty at the secret life we lead. I feel her suffering. I see her waiting for me. She puts up with all my delays and rejections. I try to reverse the roles. I suggest that she calls me when she wants to see me. I know it won't make any difference.

Whenever he leaves me, he always asks whether I need money. And I always answer yes, firmly and formally.

I have the ambiguous feeling that he must pay for the love he doesn't give me. I'm not trying to put a price on my body; it's my self-esteem that needs to be remunerated. I need damages for all the cancelled appointments, the weeks without news, the place that he takes up in my life.

I would like him to buy me so that I can justify making myself completely available to him, so that at last I have a reason to do what I'm doing.

Yesterday she broke a rule. She phoned me at home. I am cross with her. I sometimes imagine that she'll try to wreck my life. I can see her phoning my wife, my children, calling me to account. I don't know if I should make her believe I am going to abandon her. I don't feel able to abandon her.

I would like him to set me up in a flat and keep the keys. Then he could come whenever he felt like it, for a night, an hour or a minute and I would always be there for him, ready and waiting.

She said to me:

'I don't want you to go without coming in my mouth first.'

I don't think she cried, or at least no more than a brief tear when we were in the bath and she was sitting between my legs. I was soaping her back. I had made her understand that it was soon going to come to an end. Men have a hard time with breaking up. They beat about the bush. So I prevaricated, incapable of being firm. In that bath, with my soft cock resting between the cheeks of her arse, I had the feeling that we weren't going to go on much longer. She only asked me:

'Why now?'

It's true, why now?

Do there really have to be reasons?

I used to be a bit disturbed by the fact that procreation didn't appeal to me in the slightest. I didn't know where that came from. Now my best friend has just called me up. She is pregnant. It wasn't exactly a surprise. Her joy depresses me. She can't wait to see me and tell me all about it. When we meet, I get the whole lot. The visit to the gynaecologist, the photo of the embryo, the dilemma over the choice of names. Now that she's got this little one in her womb, I can't stand her. No bigger than a lump of chewing-gum. Her new condition suddenly gives her every right in the world, starting with the right to be utterly boring. Even worse, she admits it:

'Oh god, I'm so boring, aren't I?'

No comment. From the moment when the little red stain appeared on her test strip she became another person. She's a mother, a real woman. She gets on my nerves. It gives her an unquestionable superiority towards me and a completely new legitimacy. Her boyfriend – they aren't married yet – comes and joins us. He looks modestly triumphant. He tells me how the thing is developing. At six weeks, it measures two centimetres. You can already make out the head and the beating heart...

I can't remember any more after how many weeks I had my abortion. Did it already have hands and feet?

There was a point when I wanted to have a child with you. Just once, in a moment of depression. The idea of living alone with your bastard was suddenly comforting. I didn't see it as a way of trapping you. It wasn't revenge. No, it was just so that for once I'd have something that belonged to you. You've always kept everything for yourself, even your sperm.

The other day I screwed her before I caught the train.

I sat facing him. I put on my little kilt because that's the one he likes best. I enjoy our daytime encounters. He had a quarter of an hour to devote to me. He came up to the tiny room a friend had lent me. It was cold; we didn't undress. As he was leaving he said 'I'd told you it would be quick', as if he was excusing himself.

After a good fuck, I felt relaxed but also ill at ease. I am disgusted with myself for having devoted so much time and energy to it.

I am finding it harder and harder to tolerate my husband touching me. Or, to be more precise, I can tolerate it, but I no longer feel very much at all. I put up with it, like wasted time. I feel his somewhat limp penis clumsily penetrating me. He helps himself in with his finger, doesn't stroke me. I would like to be less dry. To achieve that, I know just what to do. I think of my wild nights in all those clubs where my husband will never set foot. And then I forget that this penis is attached to him, and can thus have a bit of pleasure. Then, when I come back to my senses, I'm a bit vexed to see that he has taken my sudden revival of sexual excitement as being linked to him. Afterwards, he goes to sleep or gets up to read or work. Occasionally, he fucks me from behind. He looks satisfied. If you only knew.

I don't know what I can come up with to turn her on even more. I could invite three of four friends for the weekend, and not tell them anything. She could have them one after another without anyone noticing. In the toilet, in the garden, in the kitchen, wherever. Then she would tell me all about it.

I watch him pacing him up and down in front of me. Sometimes he'll brush my cheek or my breast with his hand. He
looks at his watch and asks if I'd like to go for a drink. Have I
ever said no? It's five o'clock. I didn't know that the clubs were
open in the afternoon. Who can possibly go to sex clubs in the
daytime? Blokes, obviously. There are five or six of them scat-
tered about in the main room, all alone, all holding glasses. The
lights revolve, pathetically, on the empty dance floor. It's as sad
as a Saturday afternoon in a café in a suburban shopping
centre. We cross the room without stopping at the bar. My
presence must be unhoped-for, as I should have guessed from
the look the porter gave me. I imagine that they've all followed
right behind us, without the customary little pause, the touch
of politeness. They are all dressed, surrounding me, completely
nude.

How has this happened so fast?

Then my friends could enjoy her as they chose, together or alone. They would be free to indulge all their fantasies. She would be their plaything.

I could have her fuck a whole lot of people, I could arrange a whole lot of evenings, but I don't have the energy to do it. Her submissiveness is exhausting.

Arms hold me up, make me a living doll in their greedy hands. My fingers find straps above my head and hang on to them. I wrap my legs round someone's waist. He's behind me, he pulls my arse cheeks apart. He makes a sign, I hear the word 'condom' before feeling him penetrate me. I'm balanced on their penises like an acrobat. We're in the ring of a little circus. Two strips of low wall form a circle with two entrances that can be closed off by attaching heavy cords. I see that the cords are in place; it seems everyone is in the ring.

There are hands and cocks and me, and I'm already not there.

I remember being worried about his flight. I got dressed again very quickly, I think someone said thank you to me, just thanks, while watching me leave.

I got home early. My husband asked me if I'd had a good day. I said 'Yes' and went into the kitchen to make a mushroom omelette.

There is something exquisitely pleasurable about submission. It's hard to explain to anyone who's too rational. To be submissive and consenting does not mean losing power or dignity. Quite the contrary.

One day she asked me to beat her till I drew blood. I put this off. What pleasure could I get from hitting her?

One day she asked me to cut her with a razor and lick her blood. I thought of that on the plane. The hostess smiled at me.

She came into my life with my consent. I had imagined something else between us. I feel like I'm at the wheel of a car that I can't control. Since she's been there, no other woman excites me. I don't even know whether she excites me any more.

I did a test in *Elle*. 'Have you got the infidelity bug?' As if I needed to know. The result told me that I was 'an easy lay'. I find this description rather offensive.

I am 'at risk'. My doctor told me. Even if I use condoms when I have sex, the number of partners increases the chances of infection. I can catch the virus even if there is no ejaculation. The virus can be carried in the spermatic fluid. Condoms must be used from the first moments of penetration.

I can't manage to convince myself. Never to feel the warmth of skin, the softness of the penis pushing into me. You have never fucked me without a condom. You're not crazy. No doubt you see me as a breeding ground of microbes. You must imagine all kinds of monsters eating up my womb. And then you go soft, and my mini-skirts make no difference.

I like the feel of rubber. I like being shrink-wrapped when I fuck her so that I can come in her mouth later on. I find it even more pleasurable to come into a vacuum.

And what about all the sperm I've swallowed? The doctor in his white shirt gives me a knowing smile. There may be a risk but it hasn't been proven. It depends on the state of my gums. Do they ever bleed? I run my tongue over my teeth. Yes, sometimes.

He makes it very clear to me that it would be better to use condoms for fellatio. 'That would be safer', he says, smiling, looking me straight in the eye. This guy can have no idea what a piece of lubricated rubber tastes like. This guy can have no idea what a cock tastes like.

Since I've known her, I've had regular tests. Every time I feel the same emotion. The letter which is slow to arrive.

I run to the letter-box as soon as the postman has come. Why am I so impatient to get the answer? I would prefer not to know. That would be simpler. Not to think about it. Forget all that. My father, who knows precious little about my life but knows his daughter well enough told me that one day I'd die of AIDS. It would only be fair, right? That's what I tell myself when I'm feeling low and my life looks black.

She leaves messages on the mobile I've just bought. Dozens of them. She says she would like me to fuck her in broad daylight in a big department store.

She arranges a rendezvous for five o'clock. She'll be wearing a long skirt with nothing underneath. One seam of the skirt will be open all the way up to her backside. She'll be on the bedroom linens floor. She used that word 'backside'. For the first time she's taking the initiative. I am not sure how to act.

I'm in the Métro, looking at people. How many are being unfaithful to their wives? I think about the air I'm breathing that's already been in all these mouths. How many have sworn to be faithful forever?

I'm not really sure what I'm looking for or what's happening to me. One thing for sure: don't ask myself any questions. If I ask myself questions, I'll lose him. And if I don't ask, I'll lose myself too.

One day I remember you said that 'it is better to lose yourself in passion than to lose your passion.' You said that to me casually on the phone. It was well before our first visit to a club. You cannot know how right I thought you were that day.

I wrote the sentence on the first page of the little notebook you gave me in which you asked me to record all that I felt. A kind of diary of our sexual adventures, you said. I jotted down the sentence in the heat of the moment. And then I didn't record much more until yesterday, when you quoted that line from Serge Gainsbourg: 'Physical love is a dead end'.

I don't like writing, I prefer to talk. What little I note down I do thinking that you will read it. I don't know where I am any more. There's a force pushing and pulling me that I can't control. I feel it inside me like molten lava and I cannot resist it.

What are you going to do with all this chaos in my head?

At five o'clock in the department store, I ask her to bend over and pull her dress open to show me her arse. This she does. We eventually fuck on the fire exit up against a wall. She takes off the condom to enjoy sucking me more. I come in her mouth. I ask her not to swallow. Absolutely not.

We walk for a long time. In the cold and the rain. Now and then we stop and the sperm changes mouth. We are walking in the cold and we are the only ones to be warm.

I wonder whether our desire to fuck has anything to do with the times in which we live. There have always been whores and brothels, but how did it all work before? Were people so furtive about sex? Things must have happened more naturally. Perhaps even in front of the children. It was the Church and morality that killed off this natural behaviour and invented frustration. And as a result, punishment, perversion and sophistication. So in a sense, long live the Church! In my dreams when I was very young I remember getting very excited at the idea of sucking off Jesus.

What is forbidden has nothing to do with morality or religion. We simply change where we place our taboos, like a cursor on a scale of values, according to the period.

We fuck our way through the end of the millennium. We're lost in the new night that will last for a thousand years. Rootless and fearless, we go on fucking, roused only by the frenzy inside us. We fuck because that is how we conquer death.

I love sucking him. I know he likes it. He tells me so. I think he says so because he knows I really love doing it. Because I really love doing it to him. He must surely feel the pleasure that I get from doing it to him. I don't think I do it especially well. I can't do it as well as a professional, but I'm sure I get more pleasure from it than she would.

In fact I could do nothing but.

There is no one with whom I can talk about sex as well or as freely as with her. I could never experience that with anyone else.

After this, what could I make up?

With whom could I find this complicity?

With whom could I find again this obsessive absence of affect?

'I don't want to do it any more with my husband, you know. With you I always want to do it. There are times when I can't think of anything else. But never with him.'

'It doesn't exactly turn me on when you talk about your husband.'

'And why is that? It's you who wants to leave me, is it not?'

'Yes.'

'You want to leave me but you don't want to hear me speak about my husband. But it interests me to know that you fuck your wife at least twice a week. Everything interests me. For how long, in what positions, whether you come at the same time. Why do you think it could hurt me to know all these things? Does it annoy you to talk to me about them? Can you talk to me about everything else except that?'

'That's not what I said.'

'Everything you do interests me, even if you do it with others, in fact especially if you do it with others. I want to be your closest confidant. I want to be the one who knows you best. I am ready to do anything for you.'

'Don't talk shit. We're not playing a game here.'

'I'm not playing a game.

'Stop… '

'You're afraid and that makes me angry.'

She says that she's happy to be with me because she knows that I will never leave my wife. She says that I love my wife more than her. She's absolutely sure of it.

She is like no one else. I don't know where she gets all this strength from.

I would have liked to live this story without any emotions. To tell myself that he is just the means by which I can realise my fantasies, that the object of my desire isn't necessarily what it seems to be.

He told me: 'I don't think you love me.' A great wave of doubt overwhelms me. How do others see so clearly through my fog?

All around me people talk endlessly about love, men who go on about the love of their life, women who tell me about the man of their life. They are all too sure of themselves, they make me want to throw up.

We've got company. This is rather unusual. Our little nights out had always been secret but on this particular evening one of my friends was with us, accompanied by his wife. Which is no doubt why we came to this crappy club. No hint of dark corners for swopping, no under-dressed, over-made-up waitresses. No smell of sperm and sweat beneath the peppermint haze of air-freshener. Just people, both sexes, equally represented and not yet intermingled, who are dancing and even look like they're enjoying themselves.

My friend is a regular. He leaves the thousand francs at the door. He doesn't fuck much. He's a voyeur. His wife is younger than him. She must be near forty-five but doesn't look it. Face lift.

I quickly downed a drink and went off to dance. Was there something special about me that evening? Perhaps I was already in a bit of a trance, one which made my swaying hips enticing. Very soon I felt various wandering hands. I fended them off because I was just fine on my own wrapped up in the music. Just me with a little pearl on my belly-button, on my own private trip to the latest tracks from DJ Cam. He wasn't there and I like it to be him who directs operations. I lack confidence on my own. This went on for a short while, there were two or three of them who were trying different approaches and me dancing alone and trying to avoid them. When he came over, a space opened up around me. He'd brought his girlfriend on to the centre of the floor. She stood in front of me, her hands began fluttering over my body. Without quite touching me, she traced the shape of my shoulders, my breasts, moved down across my waist and hips, around the curve of my arse, lightly stroked between my legs, then moved her hands up across my stomach to my neck. I slowed my movements, my legs a little apart, now pinned to the spot, arms by my sides. I am now swaying only to the movement of her hands. In two steps and a few efficient moves, my skirt and little jumper end up at my feet. There I stand in bra and pants in front of this woman who was how old? Forty? Fifty? I close my eyes.

We did a line of coke. We drank five or six vodka tonics. She's completely out of it this evening. She blames me for having abandoned her for several weeks. My friend's wife has taken her hand and is sucking her fingers one by one. She does so as if they were tiny little cocks that she wanted to make come.

Her mouth has left my thumb and moved on up my arm, she's sucking me, licking me, biting me and leaving long, shiny streaks on my skin. My pussy is already sending out distress signals, demanding attention. I am aware of every part of my body: wrists, elbows, armpits. They are all directly connected to my pussy. She kisses my neck. In normal times, a simple kiss above the hollow of my shoulder, just where the fine hair on my neck starts to grow, can give me an electric shock that runs right through from my feet to my head. I'm afraid of coming. My mouth had the time to attempt an astonished 'oh' when her bites became deeper. Her lips were already stuck to mine. She was sucking my tongue as if she were trying to swallow my whole body. My pussy began to pulse like a second heart and the muscles of my thighs trembled.

It reminds me of those skinned frogs in biology lessons to which we gave electric shocks to test their reflexes. Sex can reduce you this state. Sex can be a lobotomy.

I feel happy. This little nothing that has gone into my head like a rush of cold wind has made me calm. Only my nerves and muscles are sending me signals. I am a field of pleasure.

My friend's wife kept her clothes on. She's an expert. A fine lesbian. You are lying on your back, naked, your legs pulled up on your chest. My friend observes the scene without displaying any obvious emotion. But I have a feeling he's intrigued by you. He's smiling. Like a good voyeur, he keeps his distance. His wife signals me to come over.

You come to get me after she has finished with me. Left me there, melted. I would like to keep all these marks, so that every orgasm leaves its petrified trace on my body. Then I could have them to admire, like a collection of little treasures. The whip has one advantage over the caress. It leaves a more enduring trace. The body forgets its suffering. I would like to be marked so that my body could not forget any more. He comes up and says 'Come on, we're going home' with a sleepy, contented sigh. I've never heard such an utterance from anyone but him. That mixture of indifference and attachment. He hands me my clothes which I put back on in a slow and disorderly fashion. He keeps my pants in his jacket pocket. Once we're outside, the cold revives the damp cheeks of my arse. I'll need to use all my powers of invention when I get home. The bigger the lie, the more they believe it. In any case, my husband told me that it was a good idea for me to have an evening out on Friday with a girlfriend.

My brain fried, haggard face, awash with alcohol, I prepare for the ritual. Garage. Shower. Brush teeth. Dump underwear in the washing machine. Channel surfing on TV. Sleep. 'You got back late last night, didn't you, darling?' 'Yes, I was with Gérard and his wife. We drank a fair bit. I'm shattered.'

I've learned to understand him. He is someone rather solitary and bossy, incapable of delegating except when it comes to sex with me. That's his new hobby: fucking me via intermediaries. Man, woman: anything goes. This is how he'd like to love me. It frees him from a great burden.

He'd like to see me happy with my husband. He thinks I still love him. I don't understand the scale of values of love. At what point does love stop being love, and why? And what is it called then?

I met Béatrice at a club. She likes sex. She's single, a lawyer, no children, no taboos (she says). A few days later I send her to Béatrice's place and ask her to wait for me there for a few hours. I wonder who will make the first move.

I'm waiting for him at this girl's place, smoking cigarettes and drinking champagne. She's telling me her life story, all about her bisexuality. We're drinking a lot. He turns up, kisses her, smiles at me, too complicit for her not to get the picture. I go and take a shower then wander about naked for a bit in front of her. Just so she can see. I lean down to him to whisper that I'd like to lick her. I know he'd like that. Smiling, he shares this with her. She roars with laughter. She has pretty teeth. I'm in a fever. I gingerly explore her skin, which is very soft. She remains passive, but opens her legs. My head snuggles down there while my hands run over her body. I fill myself with her smell, her sex is so tight, like a teenager's. My hands move down to the inside of her thighs and I pull them apart slipping my tongue into her crack. His gasp encourages me, my tongue laps her, at first just from bottom to top without going inside. My nose rubs against the bristle of her pubic hair, I would like to drown in this sea. When I can feel she's dripping wet my hands open her lips and my tongue ventures right down inside her, I'm exploring her, drinking her, melting into this double. I would like to make her come violently. I feel her orgasm slowly approaching and I decide to penetrate her with my whole hand while my tongue only exists for her clitoris. When her sex starts to dance, her lips opening and closing like a hungry mouth, her vagina sucking in my fingers, I experience a strange feeling of success. I climb back up her body to kiss her and make her share her scents.

Then I look at you with infinite pride.

Without taking my eyes off her, I turn Béatrice over and fuck her as well and as deeply as I can.

You kiss me and I feel a violent wave rising up inside me. It could be called ecstasy, or just happiness. I close my eyes, aware of the smile that fills my face.

It reassures me to see him so happy. He takes me home by car. There's a long silence. I am crying uncontrollably. I am afraid he's going to leave me. Perhaps it flatters him to see me so weak. I must be starting to disgust him. In the end, nothing that I am doing, nothing that he makes me do, is in the least bit admirable.

She's crying. I don't know what to say to her. I let the silence continue and the tears flow. I don't feel any compassion towards her. I do not feel I am responsible for her suffering. She chose this story as much as I did. I will never be able to give her anything other than what I am giving her right now. She's crying for herself. That saddens me a little for she is the most honest person I know.

When you told me how much you respected me, I couldn't hold back my tears.

I want time. I want him to use me for his pleasure, and thus for mine. I do not want love and above all I do not want his respect.

I give the orders but it is she herself who makes the rules. Awareness of the emptiness we're heading towards is becoming too strong. We will never be objects for each other. Yet we must reach that state. I try to tell her this. She stops crying, asks if I'd like her to suck me off.

If he had set me up in a studio flat, the first thing I'd have done would be to buy a bed. *The* bed. I would have put it in the middle of the room, an iron bedstead with a canopy and bars everywhere with coloured drapes to make it less blatant. This is not a bed made for sleep. This bed will plainly state: 'Fulfil all your fantasies with me.' This bed will be just like me when I go out in the street with my thighs still damp and passers-by can clearly read the message I'm sending out: 'Warning, sex object.' Just thinking about this bed makes me wet.

It was torture. I thought about her all the time.

I saw an old tramp outside my place. I know him, his name is Louis. He fried his brains in the Algerian war. He lives in an abandoned garage. I thought of taking him home, making him take a bath, and offering him my little geisha. No, in fact I thought that he shouldn't take a bath. I wanted him to fuck her in all the filth, I wanted to see her white skin in the middle of a heap of dirt. I wanted to see her begging me to stop. Actually, I don't think Louis would ever agree.

I content myself by pointing the old guy out to her from the car one day when we passed him. I drove that way for that very reason. I asked her if she'd be up for fucking a bloke like him if I gave the order. She said, 'Yes, of course'. That is all I need. That kills me.

He wants to see me settled, at any cost, and to be back in love with my husband. He thinks this will put an end to my suffering. He's trying to soothe his conscience. I find myself making a joke of it, saying all he has to do is find me a new husband. Less of a joke than it seems, since I am ready to accept any choice he makes for me. I wish he had the courage to go as far as me in our story. I don't want much, just that he takes responsibility for, and accepts, what I have become for him.

The detachment that he displays on the pretext of stopping me suffering doesn't convince me. Why has he still not understood that our relationship doesn't have to bother itself with that?

I've been busy with work. My wife can't get over it:

'I'd forgotten what it's like to see you up and about so early!'

I had almost forgotten her. At home I make chilli con carne and we invite Ernesto and his wife.

'You seen her again, that chick from the last time?'

I don't answer.

'Because I might possibly be interested in trying it one more time.'

I don't answer but pointedly leer at his wife's arse. He shuts up.

My wife is full of praise for the new couple that Ernesto and his shrink have formed.

Throughout dinner I think of you all the time.

I had decided we had to have an evening of explanations. Getting things out in the open. What do you want from me? I have always had very contradictory ideas about him. Several times I had made up my mind to stop seeing him. I didn't understand why I should want to see him. I ran through the list. He was nothing special, middle-aged, no sense of humour and smelled of cigarettes. A quick survey of the situation revealed that there really wasn't much left for me in this little story. And how about the sex clubs? Let's be honest. The clubs are loathsome. The stench of mint that even spreads to the street outside, the stairways lit up like some ghastly cabaret, those human monsters with four heads, those arms and legs tangled together, all the horrors of exposed penises, shiny and sticking out and swollen with sperm, and those pussies wide open and red, those breasts kneaded by hairy hands, all that whinnying, that sweat, those folds of fat, the sound of hands wanking, closed eyes, goggling eyes, that repetitive coital music, eyes glowing in the dark, this trance.

I am not a porno girl.

Do I only have my arse to offer to the world? All this sodomy, all this swinging. I would so much like to rid myself of all this shit.

When I opened the door she gave me an odd look. We hadn't seen each other for a fortnight. I could feel that this wasn't the evening for an adventure. She wore wide black trousers and a little knitted top. Very little makeup, very elegant. I got the impression that she didn't necessarily want to fuck. First we went out to eat in a very classy Chinese restaurant. The charm was broken. I'm angry with myself for not having any new ideas. We drink two bottles of rosé and some hot sake. In the car I do two lines of coke. We don't touch each other and we head off to a club. An unpleasant feeling of being regulars.

Some American hard-core starlet is on the big screen. She is trying to beat the gang-bang record. To fuck eighty-two men in a row. I leave after number twenty. I counted.

I ask her if she would enjoy taking her place. She doesn't answer, doesn't smile, looks sad and distant.

When I saw him, his ridiculous bunch of flowers in his hand, my murderous thoughts vanished. It wasn't the flowers but his presence, his scent, his self-conscious air. I regretted my outfit. I should have stuck with my thigh boots and mini-skirt. I should have made him understand that I wanted him more than ever to look after me. Impossible to imagine sleeping when he took me home at 3 a.m. My husband is snoring. I don't really know what to do, I smoke three cigarettes in ten minutes and I decide to masturbate in front of the mirror. The cocaine makes orgasms unlikely. I want to go back to the club to finish myself off with all those who stayed there. I look at myself in the mirror and quite like what I see. I revive my makeup with very red lipstick of the kind I've never used before, and decide to go back out. But I don't go anywhere, I sit on the ground in the garage and cry. I get drunk on pastis and I go to bed at exactly the moment that my husband turns round. I rub myself against his leg. I'm burning up.

Before switching out the light, I kiss my wife's shoulder.

Last night or rather this morning, I threw up all the alcohol and sperm I'd swallowed during the night.

I decide to forget. I force myself to work hard and do the cooking. Ten days pass or rather don't pass. In the end nothing really passes at all. He phones and my voice once more answers 'Yes' when he asks if I'd like to see him. That always amazes me.

What is he expecting from me exactly? I just can't work it out. His reproaches when I don't call him for a while are in total contradiction with the disinterest that he continues to cultivate in my presence.

I call her back with the intention of making an excuse but she isn't there. Just as well. I try again a few hours later without success. I tell myself that maybe this is how we can get out of it. Gently. But I know it isn't possible. Finally, one Thursday around midday:

'I missed you.'

'Me too', she says.

Shit… I promise her that the next time she will have a surprise. I decide to take her to the country.

'You took your time calling me. How long have you been there?'

'Since yesterday, I went to my parents' place first.'

'Did you miss me?'

'Yes, I missed you.'

'So let's meet, what would you like to do?'

'I'd like you to prepare something good for me.'

'What kind of thing?'

'Something violent.'

'Get ready for Saturday, I'll pick you up around nine a.m.'

'Saturday's no good, my husband will be there, but I can do Sunday.'

'OK, I'll call you to confirm.'

I hesitate to tell him again of my overwhelming desire to be beaten. I know he doesn't really want to do it, isn't sure what pleasure it could bring him. Me neither. For some days I've been developing an increasingly precise idea of what might unfold:

I am standing, my wrists and ankles secured by very tight leather straps. My legs and arms are spread wide. I am on offer. When I move my arms a little, the leather burns my skin. The first pain, a foretaste of that which is to come. I try a few movements to assure myself that I'm powerless and to arouse the fear and pleasure of absolute submission. I let myself look, some guys are starting to wank, my eyes waver over them. They don't have any consistency to me. The only thing that interests me is their penises, all sticking up in my direction.

She doesn't speak to me while we're on the motorway. We're heading for an old farm belonging to a friend of Ernesto. We'll be in one of the barns. I show her the place, the beams, the pulleys. Then we go for a stroll round. And I blindfold her. I take her back to the barn and tie her up. I don't speak. I whisper in her ear: 'So, what would you like? Tell me ...'

'A riding whip.'

After he's whipped me, he removes my blindfold. I can make out shapes in the gloom. There are three of them, wearing sweaters, their cocks jutting out, in front of me. They wear hoods with eye slits, and condoms. I am naked and cold. Their erections are all the same, their cocks standing straight up along their stomachs. I recognise his. He's standing back a little. In his hand he has a leather martinet which is serving to stoke the fire between my legs. He uses it quite delicately, dragging the strips of leather over my skin. Once in every ten strokes he gives a more violent one. That's the best, the one I'm waiting for. I must be providing them with a beautiful show. This fact fills me with pride.

Another man is hitting me with a riding crop. That's the one that hurts most. At first his blows are a little timid. I shout at him to go harder. In the end he loses control of himself altogether.

A third looks on. He asks them to turn me round. I raise my head to look at him and give him a smile. An innocent smile to thank him for finally giving me his attention. I receive a hard slap in return. This isn't a warning, it's my punishment. My eyes fill with tears. My mouth tastes salty from all the swallowed tears. Hands untie me so that my straps can be made tighter. Then comes a series of blows, the riding crop cleaving the air, lacerates my buttocks and back, the screams and sobs that I am choking back. His well-aimed, sharp blows become more and more violent, moving down between my thighs, reaching my sex.

I am just a wound.

Then they take turns to push themselves against me,

holding me by the hips to make me bend back still further. One of them shoves himself inside me violently, fucks me frenziedly. He bangs against the top of my vagina as if he wanted to run me through and only comes out in order to fuck me in the arse equally brutally. Then he comes back to my cunt. Unless that is someone else. Fucked in front, fucked behind, until my pain becomes an extended pleasure. Until, much later, I feel the sperm run over my wounds and make the pain even worse.

I didn't think I would get so much pleasure from hitting her. I could barely control myself. She wanted more. More, still more. The other two didn't go on. I gave her more than she wanted. Until the blood spurted. Until I could masturbate in her blood.

I want pain and death, to be sorry to be there, to gasp out my sobs. I want to vomit up the knots in my stomach, the guilt of living. I want to be punished.

On the way back she is more docile than ever. Her eyes sparkle with a new light. She sucks me again and does it so well. Once we get to Paris she says:

'Next time, promise me we'll try something else.'

I promise.

Why is men's desire the only recognition I feel I deserve?

I have never felt so free and also so dependent. It's really con-tradictory. I never feel like this with anyone else. I like being in these borderline states, when I feel I am completely losing control. It's compulsive and afterwards it's frustrating. It's rarely happy. It's become deep-rooted in me. She eradicates the most deeply engrained truths. We have our own laws which are not those of others. Today I'm not sure of being the stronger. With her, freedom has something dangerous about it. After all the blows and wounds, what will be next? She plays at making me believe that she's capable of going right to the end.

I would like this to finish as least badly as possible. I would like this to finish.

None of our experiences tells me anything about myself. To give up would be a failure.

I went to the little studio flat belonging to Caroline with the cut-throat razor that we use to kill rabbits. We made love. I tied her up. She begged me to hurt her. When I softly slid the blade on to her skin, I saw her eyes fill with fear and contentment.

She fainted. I took advantage of this to take the little notebook from her handbag. Then I left, telling myself that was the last time.

Two weeks later, there was just a scab left. Then a white scar. And then I phoned you. I was bereft. It's killing me, you bastard.

I went to see a neurobiologist to get substitutes. Reserved, but with a kind face. He talked about sex with detachment. He began by prescribing antidepressants. Mid-life crisis. As I was talking confidentially, I told him about you. About us. Of your wish that I cut you. That I kill you. He said I was undergoing homeostatic pressure. It's hormonal, my internal clock is out of order. We control ourselves but internally there's a merciless struggle going on. Our systemic equilibrium is ever more difficult to maintain. Chronic drug-taking produces lasting organic changes. Sex was our way of getting high. Why don't we go madder? Have you ever asked yourself that question? He explained that my brain was dependent on my muscles and my neurones and they were dependent on you. He added that only a 'psycho-moral structure' that was very strong could help us reduce our pursuit of these sensations and thus become less dependent on each other.

Come.

You left me for dead.

I wore trousers and rollnecks for three weeks. Beneath the wool I was always hot. It was good.

Come.

We lost sight of each other for seven months. I went back to writing, and went out less. She met someone else, younger than me, and also more amorous. She got divorced.

I saw her again once. It wasn't by chance. I had left messages on her answerphone which she didn't answer. I pretended to be astonished at bumping into her. She was wearing a miniskirt. She was still just as beautiful. We went for a drink. She said I looked ill. She was right. My psycho-moral structure had rallied and that depressed me. I didn't want to talk. Before leaving she went to the toilets. I followed her. On the stairs she turned to me and smiled.

Unlike a man, a woman needs time. My pleasure isn't something instant. It extends and blossoms after the act. My pleasure, it's happiness for later on.

I felt well for the first time in seven months. A strange sensation, somewhere between a light breeze and a draught. It goes by and it sneaks back, envelops you. You ask yourself whether you're dreaming. It didn't really matter that we fucked after that, her smile was all I needed to be happy.

I still wanted him but it was different. I felt detached. He followed me all the way into the women's toilets. The place was empty. I told him that afterwards it would be over. He agreed. I closed the door behind us.